BLACK RAVEN

BLACK RAVEN

DEVON HICKS

Columbus, Ohio

Black Raven

Published by Gatekeeper Press
2167 Stringtown Rd, Suite 109
Columbus, OH 43123-2989
www.GatekeeperPress.com

Copyright © 2020 by Devon Hicks

All rights reserved. Neither this book, nor any parts within it may be sold or reproduced in any form or by any electronic or mechanical means, including information storage and retrieval systems without permission in writing from the author. The only exception is by a reviewer, who may quote short excerpts in a review.

The cover design for this book is entirely the product of the author. Gatekeeper Press did not participate in and is not responsible for any aspect of these elements.

ISBN (paperback): 9781642379570
eISBN: 9781642379600

Preface

Everyone has felt like Sebastian before. We are motivated to become more powerful than our circumstances. The ambition in our wings gives us the chance to soar to a higher ascension. We want to feel the warmth of love and acceptance from all mankind. Conforming our personality to fit the needs and standards of other people makes us feel wanted. If there is one thing I learned from my family is to love my feathers just the way they are.

Being unique is ok. Do not believe you are not enough for anyone. It's fine to work and change on yourself, but do not do it for acceptance. If you are determined enough to transform yourself to better your mindset, keep working! One day, you will soar high in the sky like a beautiful Black Raven.

Special thanks to my parents: Mark and Deborah Hicks. Thank you for never giving up on me. I am humbled to be your son.

My sincerest gratitude to my little brother: Daylon Hicks. Thank you for motivating me to finish Black Raven. I am honored to be your older brother.

For all readers, thank you for taking the time out to read my first book. I love you all from the bottom of my heart. Thank you for the support.

Contents

Preface v

Chapter 1 Black Raven 1
Chapter 2 The Woodpecker 7
Chapter 3 The Buck 11
Chapter 4 The Falcon 15

CHAPTER 1
Black Raven

Once upon a time, in a beautiful green forest, hidden away from the rest of the world, all the animals lived in peace. The forest provided all the nourishment the animals needed; succulent wild berries, delicious fruit, grains, and more. The animals lived and prospered together.

One part of the forest contained a grove of cedar trees, each tall and strong. In one of these cedars lived a family of black ravens. Their feathers were as black as coal, and they had blood-red eyes.

In another part of the forest lived a family of the most vibrantly colored bird in the forest, the scarlet macaw. With their red, yellow, and blue plumage, these birds were admired by all.

Over time, some of the ravens became jealous of the macaws. They felt that the macaws lauded their beauty in order to make them feel inferior.

One young raven, rather than feeling jealous of the macaws, admired them. His name was Sebastian. Looking at his reflection in the lake, he longed for the colorful feathers of the macaw, rather than the plain, black, feathers he had been born with.

Every day, Sebastian traveled to the tree where the macaws lived. As time went by, the macaws began to make fun of him. They told Sebastian that he was ugly and that he would never have the beauty that they possessed.

Each day, Sebastian returned home, crying. How he longed to have been born a macaw!

One day, flying home through his tears, Sebastian became confused and ended up in an area of the forest that he had not entered before. There, he encountered an owl, with brown feathers the color of cocoa. His eyes were piercing and mysterious. "What is wrong?" the owl asked the raven.

Sebastian, choking back his tears, answered the owl. "I want to be like the macaw," he said. "They are so beautiful, not like me, ugly and without color."

Black Raven

Black Raven

"Cheer up," said the owl. "I know how your wish can be fulfilled."

Startled, Sebastian responded, "Oh, if only that is true! I would give anything to be as beautiful as the macaw!"

"At the far end of the forest, to the east, lies a magical fountain," said the owl. "One dip in this mystical pond and your feathers will be changed. Instead of the dull black that they are now, you will be resplendent with all the colors of the rainbow."

Sebastian, smiling widely, thanked the owl. "I will set out the first thing tomorrow morning," he said.

Then, filled with joy, Sebastian returned to his home for the night.

CHAPTER 2

The Woodpecker

Just as the sun began to break over the horizon the next day, Sebastian crept from his nest, being careful not to wake his kinsmen. He flew purposefully in the direction of the rising sun, anxious to see his dreams fulfilled.

Suddenly, a shrill cry filled the air! It came from a tall oak tree that he was passing. Changing course, Sebastian flew toward the sound.

Arriving at the tree, Sebastian spotted a baby woodpecker.

"Help me," the small bird cried. "I have injured my wing and cannot fly!"

Just then, Sebastian saw the source of the terror. A cobra had somehow made its way into the forest and was stalking the helpless bird. Thinking quickly, the raven dove toward the snake. As he neared the creature, he let out a thunderous screech, and spread his wings out to their full length, making him look much larger and far more fearsome. Startled, the cobra quickly turned and slithered away.

Sebastian picked up the little woodpecker with his beak and carried him back to his mother's nest.

The mother woodpecker was overcome with gratitude. "Thank you, thank you for saving my baby," she repeated, over and over. "Oh, where did you come from?" the mother woodpecker asked.

"I am on a quest," Sebastian stated. I am searching for the magical fountain that will change my ugly form so that I will become as beautiful as the macaw."

"Oh, my!" said the mother woodpecker. "I can't imagine wanting to change yourself. You are so brave!"

The Woodpecker

"Thank you," said Sebastian. "But if my feathers were as bright and beautiful as those of the macaw, I would be forever happy."

With that, Sebastian resumed his journey.

CHAPTER 3
The Buck

The next day, as Sebastian continued toward the east, he spotted another invader in the forest. It was a man with a rifle. The hunter was moving stealthily toward a family of deer, resting peacefully beside a brook.

Sebastian realized he must act quickly if the deer were to be spared. "Caw, caw!" Sebastian let out a loud warning cry. The strong buck leading his family turned, saw the hunter, and quickly darted into the trees, his family following. The hunter raised his gun to fire, but he was too slow.

An hour later, the raven came across the family of deer in another meadow, now safe from the danger of hunter. "I am the leader of all the deer in the

Black Raven

The Buck

forest," said the buck. "My son will someday take my place, thanks to you."

Sebastian nodded, paying his respect to the deer.

"Tell me," said the buck. "You are far from your home in the cedars to the west. What brings you to our part of the forest?"

"I am searching for a magical fountain," replied Sebastian.

"By dipping in the fountain, I will be able to rid myself forever of my ugly appearance and become as beautiful as the macaw."

"How very odd," said the buck. "Your feathers, black as night, are unrivaled in their texture. You have a pure and noble heart. Why would you seek to change yourself?"

"I desire the beautiful colors of the rainbow to clothe me, more than anything," replied Sebastian. With that, the young raven took leave of the buck and his family and continued his journey.

CHAPTER 4

The Falcon

After several more days, Sebastian, at last, sighted the fountain for which he had been searching. As he approached it, he observed a hint of colors playing in the waters. "The owl's story was true!" he thought.

As he neared the fountain, Sebastian spied an aged hawk, perching on a branch above the fountain. The hawk, even though now very old, still had an athletic appearance. His face was strong, yet compassionate. As he got closer, though, Sebastian saw that the hawk's feathers were deeply scarred.

Looking straight at Sebastian, the hawk asked, "Are you here in search of the fountain?"

"Yes!" Sebastian enthusiastically replied.

With this, a sad expression came across the hawk's face. "Why do you seek to change yourself?" he asked.

Suddenly annoyed, Sebastian responded to his inquisitor. "All through my journey, I have been asked this very question," he stated. "I long to be beautiful, like the macaw, with his rich, colorful feathers. I'm tired of the ugliness of my black feathers. I'm tired of being mocked by the macaws," he replied.

The hawk looked mournfully at Sebastian. "I was once like you," he began. He then proceeded to tell the young raven his story.

"When I was younger, flying with power through the sky, the small animals of the forest feared me. I longed to be a chickadee, so cute and small, loved by everyone. I heard the story of this fountain. I was told it would change me, giving me the appearance of that harmless, small bird, and I knew that if I could make this change, I would be truly loved. But the story was a lie. Although the fountain looks inviting,

The Falcon

it is filled with a horrible acid. It is that acid which gave me the scars that you see."

Sebastian looked on in wonder, his mouth agape, as the hawk continued his story.

"After dipping in the fountain, and receiving only these scars, I became even more depressed. I didn't know what I would do, but my fellow hawks helped me. They showed me that I had no reason to be ashamed, even with the scars that now covered my once unblemished feathers. You see, we are all unique. Some of us are more beautiful to behold. But that is not what determines our worth. It is our inner character that does that."

Overcome with emotion, Sebastian realized the hawk was right. Thanking him for his wisdom, he turned and began the journey home.

As he neared his family's tree, he encountered one of the macaws who had teased him before. "Thank you," the raven said.

"What for?" asked the macaw, incredulously.

The Falcon

"For letting me find my true self," Sebastian replied. And with that, he flew on to the cedar that was his home.

The End

www.ingramcontent.com/pod-product-compliance
Lightning Source LLC
LaVergne TN
LVHW051933070526
838200LV00077B/4639